Apple Days

A Rosh Hashanah Story

For my mother, Carole, whose life inspired this story. L'Chaya!

—A.S.

KAR-BEN PUBLISHING
A division of Lerner Publishing Group, Inc.
241 First Avenue North
Minneapolis, MN 55401 USA
1-800-4-KARBEN

Website address: www.karben.com

Main body text set in Tapeside.
Typeface provided by Linotype AG.

Library of Congress Cataloging-in-Publication Data

Soffer, Allison.
    Apple days : a Rosh Hashanah story / by Allison Soffer ; illustrated by
Bob McMahon.
        pages   cm.
    Summary: Katy looks forward to her family's Rosh Hashanah tradition
of making applesauce from scratch, but with a new baby, will the family
be too busy this year?
    ISBN 978–1–4677–1203–3 (lib. bdg. : alk. paper)
    ISBN 978–1–4677–1205–7 (eBook)
    [1. Apples—Fiction. 2. Rosh ha-Shanah—Fiction.]
I. McMahon, Bob, 1956– illustrator. II. Title.
PZ7.S685277Ap 2014
[E]—dc23   2013022208

Manufactured in the United States of America
1 – DP – 7/15/14

Apple Days

A Rosh Hashanah Story

Allison Sarnoff Soffer

ILLUSTRATED by
Bob McMahon

KAR-BEN
PUBLISHING

"What are you looking forward to this Rosh Hashanah?"
Katy's teacher asked the class.

"Hearing the shofar!" shouted Max.

"Chicken soup at Grandma's!" exclaimed Abby.

Katy raised her hand, beaming. "Applesauce," she said, "but not just any kind. Every year my mom and I go apple picking and then we make our own."

Katy had even more to share. "And I will have a new baby cousin later this month."

"Applesauce *and* a baby in the New Year?" her teacher replied. "How exciting!"

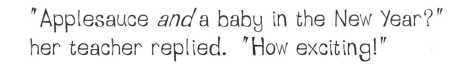

Katy loved apples. She loved biting into their crispy skin and discovering the sweet, tart taste inside. But she loved applesauce even more.

Every year at the orchard, Katy and her mother would search for the perfect apples. They would walk the rows, picking some of each variety until their bucket was full.

At home, Katy would place ten apples on the kitchen counter, and her mother would start to peel. Katy watched as her mother's steady hands moved quickly in circles, unraveling the skin like thread from a spool. Then Katy's mother would core and slice the apples, and Katy would put them into their biggest pot.

Katy would take cinnamon and sugar from the pantry and sprinkle them into the pot. Finally she would squeeze in some lemon juice and add a little bit of water. Soon the kitchen would fill with the sweet smell of apples and cinnamon. Just thinking about it made Katy's mouth water.

"Let's make next Wednesday apple day," said Katy's mother, and Katy drew a big apple on the calendar.

Katy told everyone about apple day.

Soon her dad knew,

her neighbor knew,

Carla the hairdresser knew,

and Sam the shoe store man knew.

The principal knew,

Rabbi Portnoy knew,

and her friends Max and Abby knew.

On Monday, she told her class, "It's getting closer."

Katy couldn't wait for each day to pass.

On Tuesday, the phone rang and Katy answered. "Hi," said Aunt Leah. "May I speak to your mom, Katy?"

"Oh, hi!" said Katy, "Guess what. We are going..."

"Katy, I am sorry to interrupt, sweetie, but I need your mom *now*."

Katy was puzzled. Aunt Leah always wanted to hear about everything. But Katy went to find her mother.

When her mom hung up the phone, she turned to Katy. "Your new baby cousin is coming early, so I'm afraid we can't go apple picking tomorrow."

"But Mommy," Katy cried. "You promised!" Tears spilled down her cheeks.

"I know this is disappointing for you, Katy. It is for me, too. But I have to help Aunt Leah. It's your job to be a big girl."

"But we won't have applesauce for Rosh Hashanah," said Katy sadly.

The next day, Katy's father walked her to school. "Why so sad?" the crossing guard asked. "Isn't today apple day?"

"We can't go," Katy mumbled.

"Can't go?" asked Max. "Why?"

"Because of the baby," Katy said.

Max told Abby,

who told their teacher,

who told the principal,

who told the rabbi.

When Abby got her hair cut, she told Carla,

and when Max went to buy school shoes, he told Sam.

When Katy and her dad arrived home after
school, they found a bright red apple on the
doorstep. Next to it was a note that said:

Dear Katy,

I heard about what happened.
Maybe this will help.
Love,
Rabbi Portnoy

The next day, the crossing guard handed Katy a yellow apple, and the principal placed another in her backpack.

Katy's teacher gave her an apple at circle time.

So did each of her friends. Her backpack was almost full.

Walking home with her dad, Katy passed the shoe store. Sam, too, had a surprise: a jar of cinnamon.

"Wait, Katy!" shouted Carla from the beauty shop. "I have some sugar and a lemon for you!"

When they got home, Katy lined up ten apples on the kitchen counter and tried to remember what her mother did next. She and her father stared at the apples, the cinnamon, the sugar, and the lemon, wondering exactly how to turn them into applesauce.

"First we have to peel them," Katy said, so her father took out the peeler and got to work.

"What's next?" her dad asked.

"Mommy finds recipes on the computer," Katy suggested, and climbed onto her father's lap as he searched the internet.

"Next we have to core and chop the apples," her dad said, reading from the screen.

Recipe

"Then Mommy puts them in the big pot," Katy continued. "We have to find it."

In went the apples, then the cinnamon and sugar, and finally the lemon juice. Dad turned on the stove. Soon the kitchen filled with the sweet smell of apples and cinnamon.

One taste and they knew.
"We did it!" Katy exclaimed.

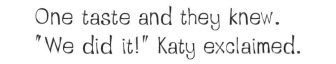

The next morning, Katy walked into her classroom proudly carrying a tray of cups filled with applesauce.

"Thanks for your help, everybody," she said.

A few days later, on Rosh Hashanah, she filled Grandma's crystal bowl with applesauce and placed it in the center of the holiday table. When her mother arrived with Aunt Leah and her new cousin Will, she hugged Katy close. Together they gazed at tiny Will.

Then Katy led her mother to the table.

"Oh, my!" was all her mother could say. Her father laughed.

There was one more surprise. Katy reached into her pocket and pulled out a freezer jar filled with applesauce. Not for now, of course, but soon enough Will would taste it and smile.

They all would.

Katy's Applesauce

INGREDIENTS
10 assorted apples
½ cup water
½ cup sugar
Juice of half a lemon
A generous sprinkle of cinnamon

Peel, core and chop the apples. (Be sure to have a grown up help you whenever you are using a sharp knife or the stove!) In a large saucepan, add the apples, water and sugar. Bring the apple mixture to a boil and simmer. While the apples are cooking, add the cinnamon and lemon juice. Cook about 20 minutes, stirring occasionally, until the apples are soft. Remove from heat. With a wooden spoon, mash the soft apples into a sauce. Chill before serving.

Note: A food processor (for grown-ups only) will help to create a smoother texture.

ALLISON SARNOFF SOFFER grew up in the New York area where she studied at American Ballet Theatre. She attended Princeton and Columbia Universities and earned a Master's Degree in Journalism from Northwestern University. She lives in Chevy Chase, Maryland. *Apple Days* is her first book.

BOB MCMAHON can never remember a time when he didn't draw, even when his teachers wanted him to stop. He received his degree in art from Cal State Northridge and has worked as a political cartoonist, advertising artist, and children's book illustrator. He works digitally, from sketch to final color artwork. Bob was also a movie extra in "MacArthur" with Gregory Peck. He is the illustrator of many children's books.